PEMBROKE WELSH CORGIS

By Rhonda E. Nichols

Kaleidoscope
Minneapolis, MN

The Quest for Discovery Never Ends

This edition first published in 2022 by Kaleidoscope Publishing, Inc.

*For information regarding permission, write to
Kaleidoscope Publishing, Inc.
6012 Blue Circle Drive
Minnetonka, MN 55343*

*Library of Congress Control Number
2021934870*

*ISBN
978-1-64519-472-9 (library bound)
978-1-64519-480-4 (ebook)*

Printed in the United States of America.

FIND ME IF YOU CAN!

Bigfoot lurks within one of the images in this book. It's up to you to find him!

TABLE OF CONTENTS

Introduction

A Regular Wrangler!

Benji barks and paws at the car window. His little tail nub wiggles with excitement. He's spotted the cows! Each summer, Noah and his family visit his grandparents' farm, and each year, Benji can't get enough of the animals!

Noah laughs and opens the car door. "Go get 'em, Benji!" Benji may be small, but he's brave! He slips under the fence and barks up at the cows. They moo and back away. As quick as a rabbit, Benji sprints around them until they're close together. Noah shakes his head. "You always have to be in charge, don't you?" he says. Benji runs about, happy to be at the farm. He looks very pleased with himself.

Chapter 1

The Story of Pembroke Welsh Corgis

A Corgi dashes after the sheep. The sheep have wandered away from the **pasture**. The sheep are used to the flat land in Belgium, not the hills of Wales. Lucky for them, the Corgi knows how to do his job anywhere. He rounds them up and directs them to the field easily.

The Corgi's owners are Flemish weavers. In 1107, King Henry I of Britain thought Flemish weavers had talent. He wanted them to work in his kingdom. They agreed and moved to Pembrokeshire, Wales, bringing their sheep, cattle, and trusty herding dogs, too. These dogs became the Corgis known today.

Weavers create fabric and art by crossing material, such as wool, in a pattern.

A Border Collie

Some Corgis still herd animals today. Dog breeds are put into groups. Corgis are in the Herding Group. Dogs in this group have the **instinct** to gather and herd animals. A few other breeds in this group are the Border Collie, German Shepherd Dog, and the Shetland Sheepdog.

FUN FACT

A dog that moves a herd over a long distance is called a drover.

A Shetland Sheepdog

A German Shepherd

Noah's grandparents needed a dog to herd their **livestock**. They have a Corgi, too. Everyone in the family is a big fan of the short, spunky dogs.

A FAMOUS FAN

Many people love Corgis, but one woman is known around the world for being a fan. Queen Elizabeth II adopted her first Pembroke Welsh Corgi, Dookie, in 1933. She's had at least one Corgi ever since.

Corgis make great herding dogs because they are intelligent and love to work. These traits also allow them to compete in dog sports, including agility, herding, **conformation**, and obedience competitions.

FUN FACT
Corgis are the shortest dogs in the Herding Group.

Where PEMBROKE WELSH CORGIS come from

Atlantic Ocean

SCOTLAND

ENGLAND

IRELAND

WALES

Pembrokeshire, Wales

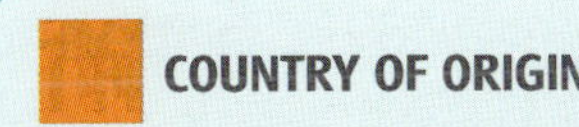

Chapter 2

Looking at a Pembroke Welsh Corgi

Benji bolts through the pasture. His **gait** is smooth and free. Corgis are bred to work. He could run all day, even on his short legs! "Benji!" Noah calls. Benji races over. Noah pets his muddy fur. "Glad to see you're already having fun."

Corgis can have many different colored coats. They can have fur that is red or black and tan. Their fur can be fawn, which is yellow or tan. It can be sable, which has black-tipped hairs. They can also have white markings.

A black and tan Corgi

MAGICAL PUPS!

Legends say fairies and elves in Wales used Pembroke Welsh Corgis like horses. In the stories, Corgis pulled fairy coaches, worked fairy cattle, and were the steeds of fairy warriors. It may be a myth, but Corgis do have a saddle-like mark across their shoulders.

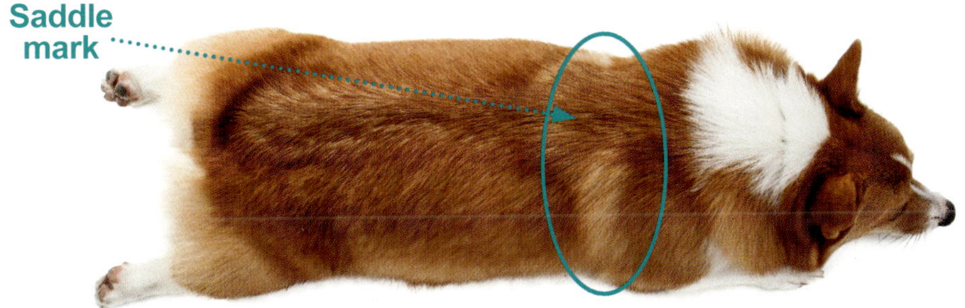

THE

PEMBROKE WELSH CORGI

MALES

HEIGHT:*
10-12 inches (25-30 cm)

WEIGHT:
Up to 30 pounds (14 kg)

FEMALES

HEIGHT:*
10-12 inches (25-30 cm)

WEIGHT:
Up to 28 pounds (13 kg)

The height of a dog is measured from the top of the shoulder, not from the top of the head.

EARS
Erect, large, tips rounded
HEAD
Fox-like
BODY
Sturdy
EYES
Oval, interested, bold, kind
CHEST
Deep, extends to elbows

A dog barks. Benji tilts his head. He knows that bark. It's his farm pal, Mac! Mac is a Corgi, too, but he's a different breed. Mac is a Cardigan Welsh Corgi. Even though he looks a lot like Benji, their breeds are not related.

Cardigan Welsh Corgis were brought to Wales by Celtic tribes. They herded livestock in Cardiganshire. You can tell the breeds apart by their tails and ears. Cardigan Welsh Corgis have long tails, and their ears are larger and more round than the ears of Pembroke Welsh Corgis. The two pups are so excited to see each other!

Corgis are short so they can nip at the heels of cows without getting kicked! Dogs who are bred to herd this way are called heelers.

PEMBROKE WELSH CORGI

CARDIGAN WELSH CORGI

- Shorter, more rectangular body
- Straighter legs
- Smaller, more pointed ears
- Oval feet
- Fuller face, rounder cheeks
- Very short, docked tail

- Slightly larger and longer body
- Bowed legs
- Larger, more rounded ears
- Round feet
- Longer face, flatter cheeks
- Long, bushy tail

Chapter 3

Meet a Pembroke Welsh Corgi!

Benji, Mac, and Noah run up to the house. Noah gives his grandma a big hug. "You remember Benji, right?" Noah asks. Benji hops up and down in excitement. Like other Corgis, he loves being around people.

"Of course!" Grandma says. "How could I forget such a sweet dog?" When Benji was a couple of months old, he visited the farm for the first time. Noah and his family wanted to introduce him to all of the different sights, sounds, and smells on the farm.

Corgis are known for the way they splay their little paws out when they rest. The stretch is called a sploot.

This is called **socialization**. When a puppy is introduced to new things and is praised or given a treat, it becomes comfortable. It is less likely to nip or bark at the new things when it matures.

FUN FACT
The word "corgi" translates to "dwarf dog" in Welsh.

Corgis make excellent watchdogs. When a new person comes to the house, Benji lets his family know. Even though he's only a foot tall, he has a big bark!

FUN FACT

Stephen King, Elvis Presley, Betty White, Julie Andrews, Martha Stewart, Selma Blair, and other celebrities have owned Corgis.

As a puppy, Benji barked at a lot of new things. He even barked at Noah's grandma! But once he was socialized, he became playful. He even gets along with the farm cat, Betsy! Now, he is a loyal part of the family.

Corgis like to work, but they also know how to play. They love to spend time with their families. Most Corgis even get along with cats! But watch out. They may become jealous if they're not the center of attention.

Chapter 4

Caring for a Pembroke Welsh Corgi

"Benji! Mac! Dinnertime!" Noah runs for the shed, but Benji beats him. He remembers where the dog food is. Noah gives each dog a scoop. His grandparents use high-quality dog food recommended by a **veterinarian**.

Noah can't wait to eat, too. Just as he's about to let Benji into the house, his grandma stops him.

"I remember last time Benji was in here. It was messier than the hayloft!" Grandma says as she hands him a dog brush and shuts the door.

"You just have to be a shedder, don't you?" Noah says. Benji just barks and wags his tail. He loves to be brushed.

The undercoats of Corgis are thick and can be hard to brush through. Some owners use an undercoat rake to keep their Corgi's fur clean.

Noah is used to brushing Benji's fur. He does it every day to keep Benji from shedding all over the house. Corgis have a lot of fur. Their weatherproof coats have two layers. This is to keep them protected in harsh weather. The outer coat is **coarse**, while the undercoat is soft.

“Almost done,” Noah says. Each day, he also checks Benji’s ears to make sure they are clean and healthy. “Tomorrow is bath day,” Noah says. Benji barks. He loves to play with the hose water. Benji can even make bath time fun!

After Noah eats dinner, he brushes his teeth—and Benji's! Dogs need their teeth brushed just like humans do. Noah uses a special dog toothpaste for Benji. Human toothpaste would make him sick. "All clean, Benji!"

After their long day of traveling and playing on the farm, Noah and Benji are ready for a long night's rest. Noah pats the bed. "Up, Benji." Benji hardly makes the leap! "Good boy!" Noah praises. He loves his little-legged friend. They snuggle into bed. Noah starts counting sheep to help him fall asleep. He wonders if Benji is counting cows.

FUN FACT

Corgis love to sleep on their backs or their stomachs. Either way, their little legs stick out.

After reading the book, it's time to think about what you learned. Try the following exercises to jump-start your ideas.

THINK

FIND OUT MORE. There is so much more to dig up about Pembroke Welsh Corgis. What do you want to learn? Find out more on the American Kennel Club website. Or look for a Corgi club in your area. You can meet people who love them as much as you do!

CREATE

ART TIME. Can you draw a Pembroke Welsh Corgi? Look up a cute picture and grab some markers and paper. Will your pup have a fancy hairstyle? Will it wear a fun hat? What is its favorite toy or game? Does it have a job? The sky is the limit!

SHARE

THE MORE WHO KNOW. Share what you learned about Pembroke Welsh Corgis. Use your own words to write a paragraph. What are the main ideas of this book? What facts from the book can you use to support those ideas? Share your paragraph with a classmate. Do they have any comments or questions about Pembroke Welsh Corgis?

GROW

HELP OUT! There are dogs near you that need care. Animal shelters can be great places to volunteer and hang out with pups. Contact a shelter near you and find out if you can help. Or can your family donate food or gear to help rescue dogs? Find out why dogs end up in shelters. Is there anything you can do to help them find homes?

RESEARCH NINJA

Visit www.ninjaresearcher.com/4729 to learn how to take your research skills and book report writing to the next level!

Research

SEARCH LIKE A PRO

Learn how to use search engines to find useful websites.

FACT OR FAKE

Discover how you can tell a trusted website from an untrustworthy resource.

TEXT DETECTIVE

Explore how to zero in on the information you need most.

SHOW YOUR WORK

Research responsibly—learn how to cite sources.

Write

GET TO THE POINT

Learn how to express your main ideas.

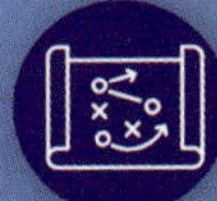

PLAN OF ATTACK

Learn prewriting exercises and create an outline.

Further Resources

BOOKS

Gagne, Tammy. *Collies, Corgies, and Other Herding Dogs*. North Mankato, Minn.: Capstone, 2017.

Leighton, Christina. *Awesome Dogs: Pembroke Welsh Corgis*. Minnetonka, Minn.: Bellwether Media, Inc., 2017.

Ransom, Candice. *Who's a Good Dog?: Pembroke Welsh Corgis*. Minneapolis, Minn.: Lerner Publishing Group, 2019.

WEBSITES

Factsurfer.com gives you a safe, fun way to find more information.

1. Go to www.factsurfer.com.
2. Enter "Corgis" into the search box and click 🔍
3. Select your book cover to see a list of related websites.

coarse: something that feels rough.

conformation: a competition to see which dog looks the most like its breed standard. Mixed dogs are not allowed to compete.

docked: when a puppy's tail is cut short. Corgis often have their tails docked so they don't get injured while working.

gait: how an animal or person walks.

instinct: a habit an animal or person is born with.

legend: a story that is part of history even though it has never been proven to be true.

livestock: farm animals that are raised to make money.

pasture: a field of grass where animals eat.

socialization: to introduce a puppy to new sights, smells, and sounds so they are used to them.

veterinarian: a doctor for animals.

Index

PHOTO CREDITS

The images in this book are reproduced through the courtesy of: Jin Ah Kim/Shutterstock Images, cover; Maximillian Laschon/Shutterstock Images, p. 1 (paw prints); Utekhina Anna/Shutterstock Images, p. 3; Guitar photographer/Shutterstock Images, p. 5 (top); Nataba/iStockphoto, p. 5 (bottom); sebastiancaptures/Shutterstock Images, p. 6; schankz/Shutterstock Images, p. 7 (top); Dmitriy Kostylev/Shutterstock Images, p. 7 (bottom); Eric Isselee/Shutterstock Images, p. 8 (top); Susan Schmitz/Shutterstock Images, p. 8 (middle); Jagodka/Shutterstock Images, p. 8 (bottom); LightFieldStudios/iStockphoto, p. 9 (top); Lorna Roberts/Shutterstock Images, p. 9 (bottom); herreid14/iStockphoto, p. 10 (top); herreid/iStockphoto, p. 10 (bottom); Veronika Kunitsyna/Shutterstock Images, p. 12; Ermolaev Alexander/Shutterstock Images, p. 13 (top right); AJMILTON/Shutterstock Images, p. 13 (middle); Kanthanat Srisantisuk/Shutterstock Images, p. 13 (bottom); HelenaQueen/Shutterstock Images, p. 14-15; Nataba/iStockphoto, p. 16 (top); Phillip Wittke/Shutterstock Images, p. 16 (bottom); cynoclub/Shutterstock Images, p. 17 (top left); ARTSILENSE/Shutterstock Images, p. 17 (top right); Natalia Fedosova/Shutterstock Images, p. 17 (bottom left); Elisabeth Abramova/Shutterstock Images, p. 17 (bottom right); Millypedwards/Shutterstock Images, p. 18; Rita_Kochmarjova/Shutterstock Images, p. 19 (top); Nadezhda V. Kulagina/Shutterstock Images, p. 19 (bottom); Natalia Fedosova/Shutterstock Images, p. 20 (top); Dan Kosmayer/Shutterstock Images, p. 20 (bottom); Melanie Cooper Studios/Shutterstock Images, p. 21 (top); Ermolaev Alexander /Shutterstock Images, p. 21 (bottom); Happy monkey/Shutterstock Images, p. 22; Happy monkey/Shutterstock Images, p. 23; Jus_Ol/Shutterstock Images, p. 24 (top); Ermolaev Alexander/Shutterstock Images, p. 24 (bottom); Bachkova Natalia/Shutterstock Images, p. 25 (top); Masarik/Shutterstock Images, p. 25 (bottom); Masarik/Shutterstock Images, p. 26 (top); Utekhina Anna/Shutterstock Images, p. 26 (bottom); Lesya Pogosskaya/Shutterstock Images, p. 27; HelenaQueen/Shutterstock Images, p. 31.

About the Author

Rhonda E. Nichols is a budding author. She loves to write about animals and all of their wonderful characteristics and survival techniques. Nichols has written narrative nonfiction series about animals of the deep, high fliers, and many more creatures, including man's best friend. Her best friend isn't a dog, though. It's an African dwarf frog named Max!